For Ben and Sylvi, who make every day an adventure— whether we're taking it easy . . . or flooring it!
—B.T.F.

For Lori and Tommi
—F.F.

Text copyright © 2025 by Bex Tobin Fine • Jacket art and interior illustrations copyright © 2025 by Federico Fabiani • All rights reserved. Published in the United States by Random House Children's Books, a division of Penguin Random House LLC, 1745 Broadway, New York, NY 10019. • Random House and the colophon are registered trademarks of Penguin Random House LLC. • Visit us on the Web! • penguinrandomhouse.com • rhcbooks.com • Library of Congress Cataloging-in-Publication Data is available upon request. • ISBN 978-0-593-90499-2 (trade) — ISBN 978-0-593-90500-5 (lib. bdg.) — ISBN 978-0-593-90501-2 (ebook) • The artist used pencil, gouache, watercolors, markers, spray paint, a drawing tablet, and a computer to create the illustrations for this book. • The text of this book is set in 17-point Futura. • Editor: Maria Correa • Designer: Elizabeth Tardiff • Copy Editor: Jenny Golub • Managing Editor: Rebecca Vitkus • Production Manager: Erika Schwartz • MANUFACTURED IN CHINA • 10 9 8 7 6 5 4 3 2 1 • First Edition • The authorized representative in the EU for product safety and compliance is Penguin Random House Ireland, Morrison Chambers, 32 Nassau Street, Dublin D02 YH68, Ireland. https://eu-contact.penguin.ie • Random House Children's Books supports the First Amendment and celebrates the right to read. Penguin Random House values and supports copyright. Copyright fuels creativity, encourages diverse voices, promotes free speech, and creates a vibrant culture. Thank you for buying an authorized edition of this book and for complying with copyright laws by not reproducing, scanning, or distributing any part of it in any form without permission. You are supporting writers and allowing Penguin Random House to continue to publish books for every reader. Please note that no part of this book may be used or reproduced in any manner for the purpose of training artificial intelligence technologies or systems.

IT!

written by **Bex Tobin Fine**

illustrated by **Federico Fabiani**

Random House 🏠 New York

Baby's at the starting gate, waiting to accelerate.

They've done their warm-ups,

checked their tires,

prepped for all the trip requires.

Now big sibling gives the call:

"Baby, start your engine . . .
crawl!"

They honk their horn and start to zoom.
Baby's on the move: **Vroom vroom!**

The best co-driver comes along,
keeping Baby's spirits strong.

Eyes lit up like headlights, bright, racing stripes in brown and white.

Engine purring, they can floor it.
Everything they find, explore it!

But Baby's in the driver's seat.
There is nothing they can't beat.

Zipping through an underpass . . .

But then—oh no! Baby's shocked!
On every side, their path is blocked!

How will they complete their quest?

A pit stop gives some needed rest.

Read a map,

enjoy a snack.

Both help Baby back on track.

Turn and loop, weave and wind, Baby wanders till they find . . .

they've made it to the straightaway!
Now what's that **drip-drop** in their way?

Slippy, slidey waterfalls...
What if Baby's motor stalls?

Drifting, dragging through the showers,
Baby uses all their powers. . . .

Engine revving, they can floor it.
Everything they find, explore it!

Then, as they roam from tree to tree . . .

...beneath a bridge,

at last they see . . .

a mountain reaching to the sky!

Baby tries to climb so high . . . .

and suddenly they're in the air, taken up with loving care.

This is Baby's time
to shine.
They've made it to
the finish line!

Parked right on their parent's knee,
Baby's where they're meant to be.

Could Baby fly an airplane soon . . . ?